101 Stories of Love

Poetry Collection

William Waldorf

Dedication

TO WHAT'S IMPORTANT IN MY POET'S LIFE

I dedicate my words first to my wife
Then per stirpes to avoid any strife
Placed in-between my delicious children
May they always enjoy beauty's vision
In my remaining days they'll treasure
Whose lives always give me tons of pleasure

Thank you Roberta, for your gift of rhyme
When an artist gives a gift they give time
From their life part of their spirit endures

My sounding boards from US-1 poets,
elliot m rubin—beat humanist
the Sunday Morning group of friends
Ann Christensen, Ginny Pina,Nancy Demme,
Joan Menapce, and Robert Berry,
Rod Richards who first heard my rhyme
And took time to reply to suggest
What they felt works best.

Thank you for sharing this journey with me

Poetry can be just two words "Me We"
Muhammad Alli, often said with glee
plus, "Float like a butterfly, sting like a bee
The hands can't hit what the eye can't see."

Poems were said when he would fight every time
A special champion beyond his fighting
gave the world humor plus fists of lightning
time showed his principals were not a crime

He spoke in iambic poetry line
ten syllables often spoken in rhyme
couplets, he preferred with their matched meter
made all listen when he used this feature
I too love rhyme contained inside our book
themes of love, tragedies turn a page—look.

A Poem Dedicated to William Waldorf
by Roberta Batorsky

The sonneteer with elegant lines
employs poetic forms with ease,
counts syllables and constructs rhymes
in well-crafted poems guaranteed to please.

A mature artist at his peak of creation
composing sestinas, villanelles and the
    occasional ode.
whose verses, arranged with care and poetic,
command we attend
a voice that's authentic,
digs deep into his mother lode.

Master of meter,
follow him on Instagram
also a mentor and teacher,
the king of iamb.

Why I Write Poetry

After I read some, or when in the morning's light
    I write,
late at night, I write under starlight, moonlight.
When rhythm and meter cede to me their punch,
as rhyme keeps time with an iambs'
    syntax   crunch,
that can only be a daily vitamin for balance.
    I write because
I remember nursery rhymes, Dr Seuss and
    somewhere a
child is hungry, and another will die.

Hope's feathers fly away from Wendell Barry's
Woodcock's quiet place to inspire. Money is not
    required
to notice beauty, love, colors, thunder, or if
    sparks fly
when childhood dreams are unleashed because
    of Mary Oliver,
Elizabeth Barrett Browning, Emily Dickinson,
    and all those
who came before and continue to write
    about young age,
middle age, old age, and other years.
Because my tears can't stop
destruction of streams, rivers, lakes, oceans,
forests, plains, mountain ranges or
strip mines, the pollution of young minds
we trap today as fish swim away with
freedoms, rights

but,
>		choice got caught
>		in a swivel chair
>		continues to go
>			nowhere
>			as
poetry workshops recite life's comradery
>			is why
>			I try.

TABLE OF CONTENTS

Prat Falls

loved to miss a desk with his outstretched arm.
he would frighten all he knew with prat falls—
shock do they sound an alarm make those calls
to 911 confirm there's been no harm

spent his life taking risk boredom not his
often waited to jump across the road
laughed at fear drivers regularly showed
all in timing he bragged to a witness

was it daylight savings caused his near miss
when his dial changed, he forgot to advance.
he fell too soon on the seat of his pants
bored no more sleeps with heavenly bliss

moral: calm adds years to many a life
try books or look to find a different wife

Happiness

happiness comes as the ambulance
screams past, to disappear
it occurs when a shadow blocks the sun
only to fade again without control
its shine proves mastery impossible

although you'll salivate for one small bite
Its return can calm your fright with a light
without a star to guide you past remorse
unable to borrow, time stays on course
if only joy could stay, a minute more

even the sweetest wine will turn sour
no more in demand, bitter vinegar
delay can offer a blissful moment
until you realize it constantly flees
from one to another, vengeful breeze

may feel like death's chilled finger calls to you
there will you finally hold happiness
but lose the scent of pines thick in the air
nature calls to sit, rest with happiness
whose many faces pass along pleasure

Alone

Stunned, I stand unable to speak or think
when love twists and turns to walk far from me.
Each step taken rips my ability
to hold on to love's pleasurable link.

When a chill brushes along my stiff back
makes me feel exposed, cold as if naked,
worthless to discard, no-one's favorite
anymore, since given such a hard whack.

When love separates, the future look dark.
Then my chest feels heavy without a spark
to make my bruised senses able to glow
when only bland sits upon my pillow.

To lose love's reply is to feel displaced
hidden, love feels as if it's been erased.

Border Watch

Simon:

There, as her hair flows in the wind--I see
my love--there, her face searches to find me
across this River Grande, her man, who waits,
longs, to wrap my arms, to accommodate
desires her smile taught to me, her lover.

Consuela:

There is my beautiful man, my partner,
Please be careful of the wire structure.
A boy was cut, stateless is dangerous.
Now is not the time to act ferocious.
Adventures like this can't last forever.

Simon:

Threat of her death, loss of my family
is why we're here now, in purgatory.
I'm still a father, a husband, a man
immigrant's a temporary plan.
Here without anything is not easy.

Consuela:

Like an eagle I study him   carefully.
My woman's eyes see into his inside
displayed to me clearly, on his outside.
To love a silent man is to learn truth
from shuffle of feet to a lost front tooth.

Both recite:
> Unable to love
> unable to hug
> able to know
> only uncertainty

Breathe Again

Do not fear change, relax, you're very young
it's not your fault in time much can be done
learn to accept mistakes, give yourself space
don't drag regret, leave it alone in place

find a partner to share silly laughter
along with a nighttime's tender whisper
study those older around you a lot
to take stock of the precious things you've got

listen as I plainly try to explain
bad times linger but will never remain
when you're forced to focus on the problem
it solves itself from newly learned wisdom

start to exhale a large sigh of relief
don't let anxiety be comfort's thief

Could This be Magic[1]

Music is love's canape' a sweet treat
or, like a bouquet garni adds flavor
lingers, but is removed before dessert
in time may become their favorite love song.

Ours doesn't need moonlight to feel complete
in its lyrics, still it's our reminder
when we wore duck haircuts or poodle skirts
and loved to dance in one spot all night long.

To look back past sixty years through a song
returns images of faded portraits
memories of a former high school lover
We still dance in place to our own downbeat.

A good cook can make flavor an experience
especially when loves in abundance.

---

[1] From *Could this be magic by* The Dubs

Changeling
(exchange of infants)

Anticipation beyond completion
waits as it gathers hope it will be loved
over our present troubled position.

Like a speck of color next to a rock
catches our eye, fickle hope flirts with time
dressed in glamour and sparkle makes us gawk,

afraid to trust desire's savory phantom
who like a hummingbird, darts in and out
in search for nectar, like hope for ransom.

Paid will satiate a promise fulfilled,
as if, and, *then* yield not to *or*, but now,
secretly hope alters, while we are thrilled.

No longer hidden, out upon a page,
my printed poems puff me proud while on stage.

Choices

Tiny child is a gift from love's bounty
fragile, wrinkled, squeaker, always precious,
requires attention, seems very helpless
will bond with a feeder instinctively.

Spreader of joy among the family,
tales of acclaim told without any bias,
sheltered, aware the value is priceless.

River of time rushes different worries
about choices, past and new tapestries
that are woven from an adolescent,
who now rejects older, wiser judgement.

Too many choices, overwhelm with stress
moderation in all but happiness.

Recovery Day One

Steps, we rush to begin, fall down a lot
but we continue inch by inch a cinch.
Upright, we learn to lean into a run
feel the wind rush past the beat in our chest,

deliberate count, one by one, on the stairs
flat like stumps fingers feel numb on the rails
climb on to the landing, to show slight smile
happiness drips no more a waterfall.

Dried sponge needs only a drop to seem plump.
Sun's rays on children's faces reveals hope
is given unselfishly by lovers.
Time stretches value's' growth with memory.

Reflections like ripples will grow fainter
as they move from the beginning of life.

Unsatisfied Breath

A woman's sigh is the ultimate high
whispered in your ear, gift wrapped in her arms.
Her soft thighs mesmerize as you succumb
to her lead, whatever she'll need to try.

A gift or prize can make you agonize
with how to apprise love to your partner,
careful, to offer, to share, not smother.
Listen to those replies and visualize.

More delicate than a porcelain vase
is a lover's heart hidden in its space.
But a flash from a fiery eye may stir
a cautious lover toward carnal venture,

to then welcome passion from another
when words bang the door of a deaf lover.

Faces of Love

Gloom day, grey day, splash as solitude begs,
while rain clouds tap my umbrella's cover.
Too many memories from a lover
whose scent of betrayal smells like rotten eggs.

Inhabits my walls to prevent rebirth
of my ability to love again.
As I walk abandoned on wet terrain
I wonder where's trust for me on this earth.

Can I find a hug to stop an arm ache
as echo repeats beats from my heartache.
I lose humor as warmth flees like a draft
cold numb like a dementor's dark witchcraft.

Love like the rich taste of chocolate truffles
as they explode taste buds into shambles.

Fire Control

Nothing says loving more than a kitchen
You can learn how to scrape burned toasted
    bread.
Distracted when the butter caught on fire,
don't panic, cover them, flames will expire.
Smoke may rise but more damage will not spread

when you've cooked your goose burnt from the
    oven,
make sure your hands are safely in heat mitts,
lower temp, open door, keep all your wits
make sure your exhaust fan will still function.

Pull blacken skin off, cover bird with juice
make it sweet. Pour all over the dark meat
add some tangy flavor like sour treats.
Now you have a sweet and sour fresh goose.

Never show the magic inside sausage
compliment it with a wine homage

Fluidity of Love

Love in fluid drops one drip at a time.
She seems nice. He is gentle, shows respect,
begins a voice for love to interject
the correct conduct for one so sublime,

captivates your eyes with his surprises
like eating or sneezing is something new.
Excitement tingles with what's shown to you
as everything often mesmerizes

until an intimate moment arrives
to pull open a curtain for your eyes
to witness a finger pushed up his nose
extracted with boogers wiped on his clothes.

Familiarity brings a relaxed state
causes the loss of a conceited mate.

Rooftop Squirrel

Along the rooftop carefully a grey
                squirrel leaps out to its
                                safety
A place free from harm
            covered in leaves keeps all warm
                hangs high from danger

where most children would go
            to find missed parents
                    after war's quick-fire fight

orphans without protectors
            stand out on
                the island of lost children

here they'll disappear
            if slow to grow up
                when alone in a war zone

where there are many
            crocodiles to fear
                who silently steal childhood

use wars to profit from
                shortages like
                        slave labor for hostages

or force employment
                of child sex slaves who
                        sell themselves to survive
war lives in never,
            never land of dammed
                where survivors know terror

What Can Happen

Yes, the sun continues its happy bake.
Sadness can't only come by when it rains,
when a thrill of birth shudders with a chill
as you learn late, its growth is a mistake.

Lost your choice locked, struggle inside its chain
as politics become economics.
Your stomach and your nausea add pain,
singled out by those extreme fanatics

whose compassion fails to help after birth,
to coldly turn their other cheek away
content to forget. but will they still pay?
Indifference breeds crime from poor self-worth.

Take care if you feel it's not your concern.
Their anger may explode from a handgun.

Socialization

solitude is like
a civil withdrawal
a whorl with wonder
desultory
hours fill the days
of aimless wander
toward sanctuary
to migrate escape
to your seclusion's
private still sanctum
for serenity

Soul Searcher Cut or Run

Gamblers when they spot a tell think it's great.
Lovers always want to meet their soulmate.
Most think instinct lets you know from a kiss,
If true, then what causes lovers lost bliss,

Violence needs time to emerge, like sauces
thicken when constantly stirred over heat.
Don't think you're broken or feel incomplete
at a mistreatment, leave this precedent.

Don't act within the soul of discretion,
expose unfaithful trolls with attention.
Two faced, they'll cower, shrink in bright sunlight
when altered from strength—
    dispose blight outright

by adding pressure on those gods of fate
Lost souls shamed, miss their chance for a
debate.

What Do You See

You can learn a lot from a pet dog.
When a wave from a tail says hello,
too tired for a touch and sniff today.
Two loving eyes never leave my gaze
as we lie and stare at each other.
While we doze together in our sleep
if I turn, a head will rise awake
not sure but ready to follow me.
When bathroom urges call, it will nudge
hard with the press from its cold damp nose.

Taught me: don't eat where you defecate
      unconditional love is as rare
       as the eclipse of the golden sun
     when then, and only then, a brief view
     will illustrate
     trusts fragility.

yes, learn a lot if you watch closely.

Make a Jump

PACK YOUR OWN CHUTE is the army's motto
A key to learn responsibility
To know it's your accountability
If your chute gets twisted, there's no hero

YOU PACKED THEM, grab those strings; snap them
out straight,
untangle those above your frightened head
Feel it snap, jerk you up like sack of lead.
Lines become taut then open the chute right.

YOUR EARS QUIET, while the ground quickly
rushes
as you brace yourself, knees don't like crunches
To absorb shock with a tuck, bend, and roll.
You'll feel the weight push away: stands the goal.

Release The Wind's Tension Pull the Silk Close
Heart Rushes, Adrenalin Flows, calm grows

Bite Your Tongue

Silence keeps tomorrow's promise, beware
anger needs two to develop its rage
or it's only a rant on a lone stage,
hurricanes at sea keep you unaware

of their destruction. Learn from this lesson.
Let caldrons cool before you'll uncover
a boiling pot to not have wound's fester
or need to amputate this blood organ.

Even if gone, your brain can feel the loss
haunted, for it knows what's the proper course
Don't stand on a rigid ceremony
when you're involved with bloody family.

Words said in anger can't be taken back
but can be muted if given some slack.

Our Empty House Seems Cold

Awoke to straighten half the covers today
poached egg sits atop my slightly burned toast,
to remind we're no longer bed fellows
I try to keep order though you're away

When the sun teases with morning shadows
My heart jumps as I freeze to listen hard
To ghostlike sounds I used to disregard
haunts the marrow of my bones when pillows

of yours, in my sleep, creep across our bed.
To make me wonder when I've long gone dead,
who'll pack memories of a survivor
alone to become the last reporter.

Those decisions may seem arbitrary
our adjoined plots will last eternity

March 1965

Through the wrong door I stood frozen since time
when the smell of sulfur brought me back, where
smoke marked my horizon, unlocked my fear,
on this lonely beach where I spent bedtime.

As dots of light pull prey toward hand thrown
nets,
out on Cam Ranh Bay[2], boys silently fish
from the end of a skiff, with a swish, splash
to pull in writhing churning sustenance.

This night's darkness lights up fear with each
flare.
Teenage marines come ashore unaware,
demons in their mind frighten some to death,
as skittish fingers take another's breath

children shouldn't play war to have to learn
accidents too, add to its confusion

---

[2] Cam Ranh Bay is now a resort in Vietnam It once was a strategic
port

Winter's Homecoming

He stretches to push sleep out from his bones,
fills the line in the aisle to become last
one in the row. His rubber legs move past
buses empty seats, to outside's cell phones.

His Army duffle rests near suitcases.
"Thank you for your service," says the driver.
His reflex reply, "thank you" is softer,
makes an about face to leave these strangers.

As snow falls spies a white owl perched alone.
Cab pulls alongside when he starts to phone
then beep clicks: leave a message
     we're not home.
Absence longs for what's missed
     when forced to roam

"Hey cabbie is there an open motel?"
HOO Blurts loud from the perched white snowy
owl.

Secrets Stay Silent

Here on the rain-slicked road a drenched squirrel froze
to hide. I panicked to view him this close,
leaped high, horror shown inside his wide eyes.
When it happened again to terrorize

me, I would recall:
suddenly visible from the jungle

a soldier, lowers his rifle at me,
pulls his trigger, nothing happens—alive.

Instinctively fire back, to save my life.

Squirrel's demise— splat. This action brings me back
to feel nauseous from my panic attack,
let's breath flow, whistle as angry horns blow.

Fear fades, no longer held hidden or close
wait to repeat my remorse's repose

Cocoon

Come close to me, snuggle within my arms,
let my body soothe away your hard day.
We lie together to start the foreplay
of our main event. Our intimate charms

are gifted to remove the world from view,
along with it, you worry not to feel safe.
For me no longer alone like a waif,
my gentle taught touches will continue.

I know you feel fragile, but you're my star.
Let's use its light years as our measure bar.
While we watch the moon rise light the bodies
we'll enjoy, like warm freshly baked cookies.
Love grows in stages, can last forever.
Sickness measured in stages reigns terror.

In Honor of Roger Greenberg

would cha, could cha, are you gonna
if I let-cha, would cha-wanna
aw come on you said you would
what's a matter   chicken?

dreaming scheming
while I'm beaming
no more screaming. just steaming
waiting for the teaching

he loved his gerunds
easy for his thinking
about matching rhyming
no longer offers   refunds

A Personal Pizza

love came to me at a pizza table
when you asked me to order, as I gazed
at your beauty, waiting tables, amazed
to see bright brown eyes stare while I grapple

with my senses, but stand out like a fool
unable to speak. Behind the menu
I nod as questions become my rescue
and time assists as I try to act cool.

My desire's wish is for a new venue
there, where my fingers can gently touch you
twist your hair aside, lean, to kiss your cheek
for alongside love there's no need to speak

Past 60 years savored chosen slices
hot, cold, young now old sprinkled with spices.

Locked In

In the quiet of the day's early rise
I reflect upon my varied replies
to times when I often acted caustic
as to burn friendships, then I was stoic.

Now compelled to face a cloudy future
with my dim vision through a deep fog's blur
lit by a glow from an ash-covered coal
my mind begins to wander as I stroll,

With my four score years towards my destiny
over those souls discarded in prior years.
They no longer wished to share my journey,
each pebble was placed down on those frontiers.

Marked by me precious but still left alone,
a cobblestone path toward my blank unknown.

Blind, I grope for your hand, my companion,
like a turtle shell offers protection.
Your past insights have been my salvation.
I fear the future without your actions.

To have the rarest gem most valuable
known to all— is your true love's gifted jewel.
Walk with me, my dear, as we share our time,
 locked together in love for a lifetime.

Hold my hand, touch me, the man at your side
and make me once again feel fortified.

Be Careful

Her serrated tongue will rip a reply
to barbs thrown her way.
She can seem so cruel
if you break her rule.

Lips become thin with a sinister smile.
She'll plot to restore control, all the while
listen politely but she won't agree
to a boundary. She struggles to be free.

Cold unresponsive aloof to others,
inside her arms she'll show me we're lovers
as her deep throated laugh signals fore-play.
In her arms she is a lover to me.

She doesn't give in, changes the subject
when you least suspect she'll call it her win.
At night she'll refuse to keep anger in.
Scent from her perfume invades our bedroom
to effect tight hugs and smiles of wisdom.

In her arms she is a lover to me,
inside her, can she feel the love I see

Night Wonders

Our moon cries at night when the sun's light
shows
its oval dark eyes, for who— new widows
I wonder, or mothers who've lost a child—
could account for his open mouth in shock.

oh, my stars, this can't be reconciled!

Forever grief will hold their heart in hock
as this pawn ticket cannot be exchanged.
Spirits miss touch when death keeps them
estranged.

Does lightning allow love to surrender?

Write A Poem

there are prompts all around us, reminders
from the past for those future new authors
props stronger than others makes them linger
as they wonder will this fit in my thoughts
for today, tomorrow, or let it stay
therein yesterday,
is it too much for them or not enough?

smooth soft cashmere of words they obsess with
again, again, and over again,
to rhyme or not is always proposed
but there must be a writer, I suppose, who'll
    reject prose
when forced to choose--curse of a poet

who counts each syllable in a sentence,
takes note of the stress from a written word,
ten iambic ones move the line forward,
a quatrain appears like sonnet's syntax

sleeps while it tosses and rolls around 'till
    smooth,
as ancestors come to wrestle with truth.

each new day begins a poet's life, some say
what will we write today?

Blame

In a fortnight, my fears might arrive here
to the experiment of a republic,
younger than most but, troubled with divide.
As sides have been drawn again to decide
if the rule of law will survive toxic
rejection of principals once thought fair.
When people of honor refuse to yield
to regroup to restate their positions
a petulant child will blame another
to learn if you kill the messenger
everyone dies.

First Day Sailors

Novice sailors out for fish in their skiff,
mornings sunlight beckons from horizon.
Out, out, far beyond the bay's partition
anticipation swells with sea's salt whiff.

novice sailors ignore: Beware of Gale
heard through static from NOAA radio.
Out, out, clouds rumble like a volcano
blue skies darken, as winds begin to wail

novice sailors feel terror from sea's wrath,
they push their way homeward in each wave's
trough.
their skiff rises, rolls, drops, to test their skill
part time sailors fight against the sea's will

Back, back to the inlet's serene water
where tired, safe, they'll share nervous laughter.

How to Make Scrambled Eggs

Break the shells, eggs are inside, be careful,
if you didn't do it over a bowl.
Mistakes teach, don't let out a groan or howl
as you learn from them to be successful.

Put a pat of fat on a frying pan–
a slice of butter, choose sweet or salty.
Melt on a low flame if it looks dirty,
possibly burned, you'll have to start again.

Whisk those eggs 'til yolks look like sunshine's
foam.
Pour them slowly into your warm skillet.
Pull from edge to center a curl's secret
for a plump thick savory layered dome.

Learn now: low and slow applies the fat's shine,
don't rush with high flame, they'll taste tough
each time.

In the Garden of Rhyme

After the midnight hour, letters flow
poetry comes alive with a phone glow
as viewers in the night wake up to write
snap fingers speak the stresses of the night

here, rhymes are tight, graphite
    leaps off the page
heaps honor out from the mouth of a sage
syncopates as it demonstrates meter
creatures who've used this valuable feature

hold power to alter all demeanor
speak fearful truth to their benefactor
hope they won't want to kill the messenger
or must they travel like a troubadour,

power of poems passed from generation to
generation
shared on Instagram™ to the delight of all
    up late at night

Empathy

Shock like a blow takes your breath, is rage left?
Pick an act. Any bat or bruise will do
Choose the cramp, the pain from another's shoe,
borrow a stranger's squeal--no steal or theft.

What can be done with it? That's a question
which encompasses your effectiveness.
While you struggle with real inventiveness
but no compassion. What is the lesson?

to heed—share emotion from another,
a required trait for any writer.
Great ones mimic; some simulate complete
sounds, often repeat them to seem replete.

Empathy, an art or developed skill
can make you hot or leave you with a chill.

Just Women

I circle her, draw near, sit where vacant,
never out of her glance, hope for a chance
to know why she holds me tight in this trance,
her moves gentle as rain drips from a plant.

Her laugh grows to chortle, we share chuckles
it disrupts desire, as my sweat trickles.
My round face feels on fire, my body's moist
mouth dry, as my stuck tongue holds fast my
voice.

Oh, to melt together like an ice block
surrenders to the warmth from the woodcock
who'll start a dance when a mate will appear
clearly, not confused by different gender

Humans lose all reason when Eros speaks.
My libido has many different tweaks
[1]

---

[1] in honor of women's month and Sappho the poet

How to Know True Love

I live with beauty not easily viewed
hidden deep along passions budding stems.
It's because the opposite world condemns
what's different. When abject fear can't include

a change. So dreaded with anxiety
when viewed it's a threat to society
though it presents new opportunities
to experience similarities.

Follow a love whose lips, though new, feel true,
strong enough to launch Troy's thousand
warships.
Learn, a loveless life offers grim hardships.
Once found, know its value has no taboo.

All love begins new; time proves it loyal.
Genuine appears after burial.

She Reflects on Age Hypogamy[3]

Surprise, love has come to me at this age.
Lonely days no longer have my todays
as I begin to plan for our future
in loving arms filled with you, my tutor.

Dark clouds drift away to leave a surprise
which fills our skies, as we survey turquoise
blue at last, it's heaven alongside you
my love, my lonely life will soon revise.

When your kisses soothe my missed desires,
I long no more as your love inquires.
Your hand on mine gently transfers our touch
which once made me blush, now wakes love's
rush.

I wonder about his longevity
when age challenges life's agility.

---

[3] **_Age hypogamy_** is where a woman is older than the man.
could be due to educational expansion and gender roles average
gap is 10 or more years

Music Critic

steady please I need a minute or three
to breathe now that you're here talking to me.
strange, I can only think *you're a beauty.*
your cheeks are flushed, your eyes reflect the
   light
sparkle, pops into my brain seem so right.

you, bubble questions like a butterfly leaps,
me I can't speak
I watch you and I'm afraid you will leave
      people should be honest. Yes, I agree
      especially to each other's sigh, **she's so**
      close
her hair smells so good when she is near me
I've listened to her music, don't dance well
why did I confess my secret to you?
no girlfriend to teach, there is only me

I keep staring when you reach across me, your
   hair shimmers,
I think you've given me nervous jitters

Love Has Many Alphabets

Where did it go? The stare I used to know
inside your eyes, now shifts from side to side.
Is it lies that replaced your wide-eyed trust
to late night's encrypted hidden text view?

Your watch glow seems so bright in the bed's light
as you sneak a peek with a turn and roll.
Late at night, I wonder who stole my role
or does *Forbidden* titillate your sight?

Do coded letters wish you to sleep tight
or arrange to meet somewhere in daylight?
Suspicious dreams haunt me at our bedside
as a phone bell's peal is softly applied,

or cursed with a torturous alphabet
when blinded by new attention you'll get.

Celebrity

I'm an ordinary man often thought
never did more than required or sought
Teachers often talk about potential
another word for possibility
after combat kept it to essential
to sidestep others' visibility

nothing special about me often taught
except control emotional export
keep to the middle to avoid trouble
don't attempt to be a celebrity
Became a set of parents who struggle
with college costs they often spent proudly

added family when daughters' marriage brought
additions from her husband's family court
forced to add more to our latest circle
against authority's ability
to be influential— is a little
one unsatisfied. who screams out loudly

became an exceptional man I think
watched to learn what I often tried to pass
did you notice her smile? No? It was gas.
Will her skin color always be that pink?
I feel a chill or draft. Close the door fast.

When she stares at me, I tell her stories.
I'm her celebrity bathed in glory

Lover's Questions

Am I good enough for you I wonder
with fear, how can I show how much I care?
Afraid to touch the answer to my prayer,
words stick inside my nervous throats structure.

When we are together the world stands still.
My heart races, my body feels anxious
as my unasked question feels tortious.
I search for courage to strengthen my will.

Life's seeds of self-doubt grow inside my mind
despite that, I feel determined
for I would feel worthless without value
if my terror will cause me to lose you

Questions never asked leave answers still masked
forever. A hidden view won't come true.

Rage from Love

nervous lonely strangers meet at a dance
distance kept while they learn from each other
shy one listens; thinks: are *you my lover?*
stolen glances wonders about romance

shy no more as lovers enjoy their night,
with secrets shared in their wished-for embrace,
sighs mingle with laughter, their happy space
often glows like a firefly's love light.

anger steals reason leaves lonely strangers
who blame another for their present state
fight their wish to hate, recall it was great
now feel dull pain from loneliness abscess

words can be an extinguisher for rage
calm, soft, bring down volume as you engage,

Rage II

control races in anger's chariot
frightened by the burst of reality
which can appear like a catastrophe
often make me act without temperate

explode frustration's fury upon all
who are near to cause them to jump with fear
when they feel my loud outburst like a spear
hurled. it can't be recalled. I want to crawl

into a hole to be hidden from view.
while my rant gives pleasure to me briefly,
those around want it to discontinue.
frankly, I want to be less angry too.

at every age, pledge to be resolute
but, closer to death, learn to *forget it*.

Love's Sustentation

when love fades away, the world feels broken
unable to heal, like cuts feel open
throbs in saline help, help its pulse driven
each beat longs for relief to be given.

look around, you remember it was here
but your eyes didn't see it disappear.
you look again, slow, is it over there
where a scent still hangs in the atmosphere?

brief bliss as you inhale? can you recall
what love felt before you had this trouble
or conflict from different changing pronouns?
learn how to overcome their rift's meltdown.

know most obstacles can be averted
when all genders are always supported.

Unwanted Guests

Grief came for a visit she didn't call,
plans to stay forever although implied
she must've come hidden in all those cards,
the happy ones that you thought were so crass
left out open scattered on our table.

No, maybe it was when the door opened
as strangers came inside to pay respect.
Wonder how much change will occur in me.
I've learned their price--pieces from my bruised
heart.

Visitors fill cups to drink from this house:
The mourning mansion that serves *please not me*,
coffee, milk, tea, along with strong whiskey
to blur away both day and night quickly.

In the silence I think Grief stole our laughs,
took the noise away, left the loud tick tocks,
to think how long before we're together
as grief accompanies my shower cries.

I bury my sobs inside our towels
to remember our spoken solemn vows:
our love will never die my sweet beauty
but be together for eternity.

Jazz Repertoire

From an aged casket
you sip the smoothest
hold the glass to light
study its color
taste its rich bouquet
raise up to salute
the one Lady Day
an ultimate muse
teaches the blues
today on her Birthday
April 7, 1915, listen
don't think, drink

No Words

Pain makes cowards of any strong being
when love shows its limits, and you suffer
openly, I struggle for a buffer,
unable to relieve what I'm seeing.
Love learns to share with each touch provided
secrets confided as fears are nurtured.

Fright grips my ability to function.
Frozen freezes my chance for reaction.
I offer touch when you ask: *squeeze me tight*.
I reply give me your pain. It's all right.
Inside my soft gentle embrace is calm.

As I pull against your warmth and marvel
how secure we seem with every exhale
to become one spirit within our form.

Touch is Our Greatest Sense

I watch my love walk away and wonder
about whose power keeps us together
some subtle gifts show hints of mystery
like a playful smile displayed cheerfully

touch is what I always thought holds us close
a head gently pressed upon a chest knows

the twirl from your fingers among my hair
a pressed ear can hear me breathe in shared air

I can feel your hand squeeze my bum's cheeks
tight
spider-like tactile chills tingle, each night

touch ...

anticipation rushes my heartbeat
imagination starts libido's heat

your touch ignites those flames eager for it.
ready to initiate our favorite--

additional desired orgasm
as displayed from past enthusiasm

touch is power inside or out lover
No one will argue its value forever

relief applied from a gentle massage
offers calm or Chance's proven recharge

take my pain, depression, anxiety
hold my hand, wrap your arm tight around me.

Sleepless night as you fight for our

covers, only room for one.
When sick space is scarce,
rest is precious. Then I flee to our chairs
where my love's gift is my silent gestures.
A damp, folded towel for your warm head,
too tired to notice— you fall back to bed.

I replace covers you kicked to the floor.
When I wonder if I can do some more?
Notice my breath soon matches your rhythm
as I quietly help with each inhale
to hope my prayers for good health will prevail
because tonight's open mouth looks gruesome.
In sickness or health, your serenity
is secure when a love is primary

Dream Ride Home.

Red spiked heels she wore as she smiled, tired
it appeared in the early morning light.
A white fox stole was wrapped around her tight.
A club dancer by her dress, I wondered
Why this bus, as my fantasy blows up.

She fights sleep with each bounce; her head bobs
up
trance-like eyes close, open, close, fight
sunlight,
as her head flipflops each time she's upright.

Bus screams stop; back door brings in outside
cold.
Waitress in navy wool coat leaves with stole
framed like a picture through the rear window
shows a missed chance to know a lover's role.

Together they walk up their avenue
while I ride toward fantasy's rendezvous.

Limbo

No place to rest either too warm or cold
as you pull or toss away your covers
unable to find a place for illness
relief. A sheet for your back has one-fold.

Too high or too firm, none right as you squirm,
moan low throughout the night, to reaffirm.
Distress can test love's limits each hour
as senior muscles will ache when mature

Touch is what a love offers to soothe pain
when skin feels the shadow before the brain
gives relief, cools then warms from outstretched
hands.
Offers skin's magic to still loves demands.

To have love is to have a place for calm
as cold hands become a lovers' warm balm

Oh No

Terror rushes as your outstretched arms flail
unable to stop your descent. You fall
with a thud as you roll over to call
for help, look around for a support rail.

Someone shouts *are you all right*, as you cry
angry tears and your fear's kept well-hidden
when helpers come, to want to know answers
about your condition: You will modify

the seriousness, afraid you can lose precious
privileges most seniors' desire.
Like scents fade from a bakery capture.
Never will you guess what old age values

until you learn what you took for granted
becomes less as each year is acquired.

Grandpa Love

Doesn't know words, or melodies, but sings,
babysits and resists an urge to sleep,
folds cleaned laundry places them in a heap
knows ice can help sooth sore gums when they
sting.

Wonders how he lost all his energy,
his legs longer, but babies seems faster
as they crawl out to a candy wrapper
left on the floor with no identity.

Stares in wonderment at his wiggly one
who got his love from the day he was born.
Mother-daughter teach father their new way,
but he knows love is still shared the old way

with a hug or kiss, a tickle can't miss
as generations enjoy their new bliss.

Sad Poems

don't read your sad poems to me anymore
my heart is shattered apart with our loss
quiet haunts inside my brain *times* the boss
as here I wait to hear about a cure

don't be dramatic, it's one weekend
you say, *bake your pies, don't catastrophize,*
our dinner's here, let's organize,
remember your grandchildren will attend,

why are we the parents who bend's each time?
Pop-pop I love your apple pie they say
laughter chases my anger far away
cherub smiles, sticky faces can't hide their crime

spent the hour deep in children's chatter
worn out, fell asleep my poem will keep.

Love in An Isosceles Triangle

Love gathered through the years is familiar
until overwhelmed by an equal side
who attacks without regard to their pride
each side's an objective in this warfare.

Here, the battleground is always unsafe
stand left miss the right on a moving train,
stand right miss the left, fear torments your brain
as two loves two sides to protect, will chafe

excitement down to feel like a prison.
The only key is rubbed rough from worry.
Vanity wants pleasure not misery.
This view the braggarts never did mention

Words must be used, love is like a river,
don't doze, as it flows, share avoids failure.

Choose Your Choice

I didn't know I didn't understand
afraid to yell your body hurt my hand.
heavy weight when your knee forced open thighs,
as you ignored cries, please, pleas became sighs.

I didn't know I didn't understand
why you did this, pushed you off ran, ran, ran
into my shower glad to be unseen.
rage at being used, abused, felt unclean.

I didn't know I didn't understand
felt my life over too naïve to plan.
want to keep it a secret tell no one,
afraid pregnant will show to everyone.

I didn't know I didn't understand.
throat sore since you held me tight for control.
repeats daily rage, rage, rage with its throbs.
painful chest sobs steal my sleep my self-worth.
I didn't know I didn't understand.
just sixteen locked in the law of the land.
no advice allowed from medical docs,
those sympathizers will be put in jail.
I didn't know I didn't understand,
echoed over and over in my mind.
no-one can help. I'm the one who has shame.

strange calm overtook me before the train. beaux
mort

Baby Cousins Together

I needed to know why we haven't
heard from my younger cousin Vicki.
Afraid to face death resisted the call
"I'm phoning Francine her daughter,"
my wife said. I listened to the one-sided call,

She's where ... brain tumor ... cancer ... we'll
come
overheard overwhelmed with back flashes
of childhood swims in an aluminum tub,
moved to different high schools, lost touch,
football rivals see you're a cheerleader

Still cruise together along the avenue,
cheerleader boy magnet also draws girls.
Married to your west point soldier you leave
for Germany. Come back with three children
but it's like time stood still and you never left.

Grey haired beauty holds my hand as
I sing football fight song "this is the day
we meet the foe"[4] brings out a smile.
gets another when I repeat eh rah eh rah
push 'em back wa-a-ay back, we laugh
but no sound comes from her wide grin.

I hold her hand through the hospital
bed slats while I try to keep her awake
leave to get dinner Francine calls mobile,
no need to return home. I remember
still wonder how long before we're together.

---

[4] sung to Notre Dame fight melody

Desire

I must see her again and hold her hand
in mine to feel the softness of her touch
which intoxicates my heart like a rush
as anticipation strengthens demand

I must see her again, make her my wife
life without her at my side is lonely
only her love can make me feel mighty
sincerely accept my pleas for no strife

I must hear her giggle, see her smile
as our hearts share love and want to marry
If I should lose her, it fills me with worry
a life without her is to know exile

Like a forgotten plant often wrinkles
to contain sustenance lost from small dribbles

To Granddaughter

My face overflows with smiles
   I write to you
Giggles in my arms I hold on to wind
   I feel love
Eyes flash me a look, my heart smiles back
   I know love
We play pretend, share imagination
   I share love
Stories and pictures forever for each other.
   My gift is love
Pinned to our hearts never apart from our past
   I love you
My arms wrapped around for comfort
   I soothe love
When I am gone you will have known me
   I left you my love

Let's Meet for Lunch

At our park, I watch heads turn all about
to nervously search for their lover's face. Lunch
begins with a hug as hands embrace
eager to fulfill each other's take-out.

I watch as novice eyes smile with ardor
a look I once shared with abandon, too.
They have a love held only by a few
no longer strangers, they share their answer.

I still remember when we were brand new,
safe within our snug space, wrapped together
intimacy shared and held by we two.
Strangers no longer, love gave the answer

I sit in the park at our favorite spot
with memories of my deceased sweetheart.

An Ear Worm

Damn, you'll get over it, we tell ourselves,
move on, it's not bad, you can ignore it,
don't obsess here, pick out another view.

Did Dodo Bird[5] understand but forget
'til soon there were none. Rockfish get a break
with one-fish limit. Sailors are upset
as *let me think about it* spills from phones
of charter boats whose captains loudly moan:
We may be gone one day from Chesapeake Bay.

It's an old story being repeated.
Forests will deplete and *get over it*
echoes in your brain.
Get over it; get over it will reign
when obsolete instinct becomes extinct.

To not even feel the weight from a shroud
alone and without any support crowd,
get over it tortures a cancer ward
when a prayer asks for additional time
to be around long enough to be bored

---

[5] extinct species

I n t i m a c y

is more than a caress
or a touch when you're near—
words aren't needed
for a love's wish

it's strong, like friendship
adds the ability to anticipate, not
hesitate, to share

the brush of hair away from your face
to sense you're cold or warm and be there
in your space with a kiss or hug

when hungry or tired and know what's
preferred from a look or a shrug

to be intimate is to give to you my love
warmth like a soft glove holds tight

and offer laughter on a sad day
to comfort you with my care

From First Flutters of Love

To young lovers unsure of desire
I shared some doubts like you, I had them too,
only to learn, love took some time to know
though I'd inquire what it would require.

The day when it stood inside my doorway
an unsuspecting day of affection,
it selected you as my companion
when on that day you took my heart away

destined as I casually took a ride
with a friend who suggested that we date.
Sixty years later some will say that's fate.
Imperfect our supportive source of pride

for we elderly with our memory
know that true love's reveled trough history.

Among Stones

I walk in open fields bordered with trees.
The ground is covered with past fallen leaves.
Songbirds announce my presence on this day.
Missed you and thought, *I would stop by today.*

There's a chill in the air as clouds gather,
I turn my collar and hear thunderclaps.
Heaven's tears begin to drop on my cap
as I stand at your headstone and chatter.

Talk about what you missed the week before
pours from me as love continues to reign
even though you rest alone in your lane.
I stooped to whisper, *you're the one I adore.*

A half's, not whole when love's partners must go,
the survivor resists letting them go.

Desert Story

The desert rodent and the horned viper
locked their bite, unable to make a change
from their guerilla tactical exchange.
Reason flees when freedom dies from seizure.

Each, afraid to yield an inch like statues,
stand their ground throughout day and night
venues.
Moisture flees; life is of little concern,
baked in the desert like toast forgotten.

It dries inedible— a hard burnt taste,
others want to teach this generation
without concessions, death joins the stubborn.
Be slow to use war, grab for peace with haste.

When an omnivore meets a carnivore
consumption continues for forever

Female Poet's Sight

A gifted or cursed body, this woman
I dislike the vision that lays before
as I drink it in, devour each line,
inebriated eyes show he'll ignore

I'm only a tool for his desire
used surrendered, savored repeatedly
until placed alongside, reluctantly
drained from the wait when my body's trigger

will spark, illuminate a dark tunnel
bright enough and able to rekindle
warmth from this lover's heated crucible
here we could grow to become a couple

his bodyweight raised, to avoid a crush
but will feel pain from my nails with each rush

In Her

There's beauty without motion's when women
like the graceful curve from a swan's long neck
displays peace like a serenity's check
as they glide along a surface. Even

when they share colors which brighten the skies,
like the glow from a red sunset glimmer
can make hair shimmer and your heart quiver
such beauty is why you'll know they're a prize

When hips undulate Ike the tides motion
alternate from side to side all women
release their beauty. When a simple gait
draw looks like a flower's perfume says bait,

to not have a female relationship
is to not enjoy beauty's craftsmanship.

The Invitation

Dust floats inside the sun's rays to expose
blurred blue ink on a folded note paper's
open flap, which lies on a wooden tray
with two half-filled red streaked wine goblets.

A short shade pull gently rocks to and fro
from the breeze of an open window's blow
Women's clothes neatly folded on the chair.
Recliner has others scattered about

wristwatch on table next to bed vibrates,
towel wrapped middle aged man scoops it up
fastens to wrist gathers clothes strewn in room
a wrapped towel headed women enters the room,

gives face make-up a glance in the mirror,
straighten skirt, checks room, buttons up her
blouse,
pickups blue note card from wooden table,
slips into her purse retrieved from chair.

On tips of her toes, without heels, they kiss
a peck, as he turns to leave feels a tug
from his sleeve which demands more attention
longer kiss as he places envelope's remuneration

alongside a crystal vase that holds one rose.
Alone she holds that rose against her nose
as pulled petals and tears fall to her toes.

Mirage

The tire looks low
I call road service
no loss of air—told
the gauge number's
correct

It must be filled
with doubt
as each time I drive
it asks me to look
makes me uneasy

Quick Choice

I stand in front of an open refrigerator
not able to see but feel the cold air rise
as I bend close for inspiration

What to pick? That piece of fruit?
 In season peach looks ripe outside
    but: last was mealy, stringy

It should be clear you choose pleasure
  Nothing is easy, everything has consequences

Adultery can feel like an unwashed peach

Right Before Our Eyes

I love it when rain pockmarks dusty ground.
Kerplunk scatters dust like seeds in the wind.
Pelts fall as raindrops moisten unassigned
terrain like a sponge swells up to rebound.

Water drops gather in a depression
to gain in size before their possession
of dirt, as streams stretch for their survival.
Dust displays mud, wet, thick, soaked, magical.

Transformation allows life to begin,
within and above its moist, rich border
proving the ability of water
to nurture again, and again to win.

Without water there is no life, but dust
needs this solvent to offer an assist.

Hard Standards

Up and down the painted horses go round,
pass the gold ring dispenser feel the sound
and watch the rings slip away from fingers.
A life filled with jinxes is where I'm bound

up and down on my horse named loneliness
I watch gold rings continually fly, bye,
unable to take chance and will not try.
I live with failure's friend called hopelessness.

Up, down are my comfortable results.
Changes would challenge my old behavior.
No disaster affects my composure
as these can only bring shouted insults.

When the image in your mirror is new
and frightens, you'll yearn to keep your old view.

Bonding Through Cloudy Glasses

Saturday, we leave in the dark,
a day with Dad at work. We drive
45 minutes in silence, to the Green Diner where
my breakfast pancakes wait. He introduces his
"kid" to the waitress, cook, and cashier.
Before we leave to open his tavern,
I watch his reflection in the car window
as unfiltered cigarette smoke fills it.
     My father's lungs
        wheeze, gasp, bring tears.
In the bar:

    a clean white apron is tied under my arms.
    As stale beer joins sour air,
    I fill sinks, gather glasses to soak,
      lift up floorboards
    to brush away yesterday's debris today.

I continue his check list:

    look at kegs' levels,
    hook up new drafts
    if needed, and do final sweep
    before tavern opens.

Now I can sit at the bar, like the men, and eat my
lunch.

I'm driven to the movie theater where I watch
cartoons, Flash Gordon clips, a yo-yo contest,
plus those two hour double western features

without family, friends to share popcorn in
Bayonne New Jersey
recall his boast,
'bout bonding time.

Breakfast News Watch

With morning light, I watch the sky wake up
in the land of watchers. I view my screen,
crack my eggs over my sizzling butter,
watch a map show today's change in weather,

slice my muffin and place in a toaster
BULLETIN, BULLETIN blares from the phone.
Possible Hate Crime scrolls across my screen
red letters flash while I spread my butter,

Commercial Break as a beer bottle shakes
Watch a young man carried by ambulance
somewhere away. Today he's evidence.
no longer a child, bullets chose manhood.

Eggs flip and yokes show their thin rivulets
to mimic my previous exhibit
Anchors weigh me back try to entertain
but I can only scream at today's screen.

Hope

when a glow from a cheek will quickly fade
as lips tighten with determination
or a slight smile shows its apprehension
then you'll pray hard to keep its flight delayed

you're afraid it may be frightened away
in that prayer you'll ask, please help in some way
but like morning haze when it disappears
hope's a butterfly who briefly appears

it lights upon one stem before it flies
to another, to rise and tantalize
like a prize sometimes can tease your desire
and you'll long for your loved one's lost whisper

if clouds are the darkest, hope quiets fear
often, it appeared, from that lover's cheer

To Feel

To feel beauty shine like a symphony
can make my heart weep from such harmony,
or feel along my neck's base, a tactile
brush so faint; my hair begins to tingle

between shoulders, to release a shudder
of emotion along my vertebrae.
Sensual sparks come with this interplay.
It's my moment alone, like no other,

to feel love's sounds inside my heart react
in such lyrics feels like love poem's syntax,
a mix of natural rhythmical melody,
like the ebb and flow of the rolling sea

becomes my own wondrous arousal,
when immersed inside our cherished cradle.

Who Loves You

My love will get roses from her lover
on her birthday, and he will watch her smile
feel her warmth from a hug, all the while
realize how lucky there is no other.

He feels her hand on his arm for balance,
upset he can't do more at age eighty.
his gait is shaky, but he loves freely
as he continues to offer romance.

Worries who'll be here tomorrow
to enjoy sharing her last crescendo
filled with harmonies from life together
and their shared sixty-year love adventure,

or will she rest comfortably with me,
finally, her lover for all to see.

La petite mort

Time concentrates from a week to a day
within it there are twenty-four hours,
each hour or a minute is for lovers
sixty seconds is needed for foreplay

Seconds, will flash then a body can know
pleasure beyond movement begins to grow
a brief shudder as your tensions release
tight muscles while you absorb fantasies

Press your source, afraid you'll lose the sweet
spot
as it fades, you'll desire to repeat
willing to remain in this trance like state
when your tongue licks chocolate drops from your
lip

and pleasure replaces reality
as seconds feel like an eternity.

Parental is Perennial

From puzzle blocks to playing hang-man games,
hours spent bubbling imagination
secretly slipped inside your brain, a ton
of memories although can't recall names.

Images flash back to our high five slap
none come from the crack of a swinging bat.
My intern has joined his beginning team:
talks of work, lunches, my eyes proudly gleam.

Yes. Pop-Pop, I'm getting paid, he replies
me too echoes inside to shared high fives.
wiping a tear from the side of my eye
No, no it wasn't too hard I reply

Hardest love to give, needs a step away
to admire beauty in love's bouquet

Stare for Clues

I'm half not a whole when no-one's here.
My disability costs a "bankroll"
which I can't understand. Much is not clear,
Hard to be special, constantly struggle.

Life on the spectrum is seldom easy.
Literal misses, subtle suggestions,
unable to hear those voice inflections
makes relationships at first feel shaky.

Since most will require more directions
to satisfy my new friend's proposal
who'll think hesitation is disapproval
before I'm able to show corrections.

Non-verbal a difficult dialect
to know or show when I try to connect.

Senior Moments

You can't be alone. What if you fall and can't get to the phone?
Assisted living always has someone available we're told
Past space too big to upkeep, you'll need to downsize.
Remember, we're only doing this for your own good.
You live alone. If you fall, then what would we do?
You're not able to cook anymore. They'll do it.
No, don't do your laundry, they'll collect it.
Not a lot of room, but enough for you.
Closer, it seems walls can shrink in
Here, a chair, bed, and window
offers a view that can't fall
You're older and fragile
sit on a bed, chair
See from there.
like a grave
Sign now.
Bye.

Where Did They Go

once laughter filled every room in my house
time has thinned those story telling jokesters
who lie silently without responses
still, the dead's stories linger like old vows

who will be at my funeral I ask
make it a grave side service some suggest
stunned this is my reply: where's all the rest
of my relatives, lost now's a tough task.

it's a lonely cold place there's no laughter
heard unless brought here by a visitor
who comes to confess, a better wish is
come see I've lived to earn a late finish

only to find its lonely at this end
scared anger shook all down to the last friend

Self-Taught Artwork

Doctors are taught how bad news should be
brought
When you stare into the face of terror
You think it will remain there forever
with those words held prisoner in your thought

a child learns mother's love is ageless
it is a taste that won't be forgotten
returns when death visits the disheartened
it can restore their mother's gentleness

like a soft caress on a lover's cheek
tells all that the distressed will need to feel
no words as they no longer need to speak
each has learned how another can reveal

when touch has become their telepathy
thread through time to weave their love's
tapestry

Once There Were Many

Les fleurs d'amour crowds tight when in a bunch
Like grapes cluster together may display
Abundance before you'll know consequence
One by one plucked until they faded away

Lonely makes me think of her all the time
When I was afraid to let her be mine
Content to resist a love from divorce
Whose source could be filled with daily remorse

Leaves both to question lovers' behaviors
Having witnessed both their acting careers
Flowers will wilt as they evaporate
Love begins to die when guilt permeates

Few tears if never allowed to get close
arm's length love knows how to dispose

Standing Alone

You remember the sting of being last
to be picked when you were not near the best
childhood sports assaulted your self-worth test
one by one others left you the outcast

will I even get to play you wondered
quickly total all the others standing
no more chosen by default you're covered
happy to play position called dumping

here the sun beats down as bees buzz around
content for their company you choose all
pick a dandelion to stick on your cap
but never don't ever, sit on the ground

home is where they will always take you in first
relieved to have a place when you're the worst

Cars, Cars, Everywhere
what color do you choose

To zoom here from there fast, gives all a thrill
wheels have replaced legs for faster, sleeker
strategy, bling creates a desire
to choose it for your new automobile

Key Fob in hand, age no priority
first time begins familiarity
no used car scent still you slide in this one
All breeds fill greed's lust for speed as you're
drawn

past puberty into adolescence
Encounter quick skids; you'll lose your control

Don't act too bold, or anti-lock takes hold,
it's pathetic, 'lectric ones as silent as

horseless buggies, driven gasless
but aggressive drivers are still reckless

Smokey Says: Beware of Feeding
Frenzies When Home's a Zoo

Learn about monsters my young, little boy
Zoos separate animals from humans
Bears stop their roam once they find provisions
Unafraid they'll return to continue

Park rangers know this circle of horrors
Can only be stopped when it is broken
Evil lives in caves of the unspoken
where heinous acts occur with callousness

Who's more in danger in an unlocked zoo
our battered woman's child when there are two
no-one believes victims will ask for violence
wear wrong clothes or have the wrong
appearance

ask why these replies blame only victims,
defenseless prey, whose cries can't or won't
breach eardrums

Time Haunts Me

The clock over the kitchen table just stopped
Changed battery but no minute hand sweep
No movement I'm unable to start sleep
but began to think maybe it was dropped

Had to buy online, since stores don't feature
It will take three days to arrive right here
when it fell off my wall, must've lost gear
Sat above a butterfly-framed picture

What's my choice I asked a horologist
to help find proper size to hide this space
which pulls my compulsive repetitive gaze
to it each time I sit to eat at breakfast

and watch how time dictates my behavior
to rush   or eat slowly at this hour

Wonder Begins

When love begins to grow your heart will know
how to tell if it feels safe to follow
loves aura when you're pulled nearer to it.
A rose scent can't be held, still you smell it

feel its presence, all around see its vine
yet unable to hold its scented air.
Nature may show to you your love's eyes shine
when they watch with hope at your open pair

to find freshness in a coy smile displayed
as your nervous heart flutters now afraid
your butterfly may flitter far away
you must begin trusting what's presented

flowers begin to slowly show beauty
love nurtured yearly gains intensity.

The World Feels Light

My heart feels the wings of laughter take flight
as I become giddy from your sweet love
unable to think beyond our next hug
scents of your freshly washed hair, skin so tight

I cannot resist. Pull me to you, close
overwhelmed, I fall into you— dizzy
inebriated by love, I'm happy
as we embrace, your cheeks blush like a rose

my ears hear our shared laughter all the while
glimpses reveal your grin's become a smile
then my heart rises to feel overjoyed
as you beam proudly at me— your reward,

now. locked tightly in your desired embrace
don't be fearful, love doesn't want to escape

A Gentle Leaf Warmed

A man's arms open to share warmth when cold.
His chest, a place to rest your head when sad.
His love to take hold as you both grow old
whispers being close to you makes him glad

disclosed nerves fear you might reject his wish
make him lose his voice as he prays for choice
to go his way; frantic you might vanish
from his life, this boy feels his heartbeat's noise

as seconds fall 'till you lean into him
smell his scent, feel his pressed hand on your
    back
gently held for him love is not a whim
hear his sigh of relief as you go slack

in his arms you feel him shake with relief
rub his back, dry tears, begin a new leaf

The Sidewalk. III

You who told, of those who belittled, scorned,
molested, you, who told of those who use their
positions to subject cruelty and perverse desires,
you who've told, of those who still remain
    in power,

Have you returned arrogance with pretense?
How many years, days, and nights did you spend
hating glaring, despising with merciless
heartless remembrances?

Let's walk over concrete sidewalks,
sit down, on the cold
stone the stone cares nothing
about you, it doesn't want anything from you
    it lies
flat gathers cold.
Stone,
it has its own purpose to be itself, to let stone
be stone
let the sky be sky to let girls be young girls
freely—
let a middle-aged woman be, comfortably
a woman.

Those past bloody nicks and cuts—endless
calamities of your battered past— *Feh!* disown
them from your life; use what's left to enjoy the
rest.

Strangers/Novice

I have seen you walk off the train with me
each morning, I watch you walk and wonder
how to become closer and a lover
or talk with, I'm single and know lonely

With your name, I could whisper *"I love you"*
when we'd lie close enough to share our day
we'd smile like yesterday blew me away
when together under the track walkthrough

I offered you my hand to help you climb
and yours steadied mine, nervous with my fear
 I wanted a plan for us to spend time
and stop you viewing me as a stranger

I blurt out:
    "you dropped this handkerchief, miss"
purposeful or not since I'm the novice

As Autumn Winds Blow

Another doom and gloom poem is being read
Each syllable fights like when a dull knife
grinds along the edge of a stone called life
words balance, with meter as their imbed

steel curls, each pull to an opposite edge
over and over back and forth to snap
then continued with a smooth leather strap
is this what we did to our marital pledge?

You said I wasn't aware what I've done
Blame fluttered like wings, and soon flew away
but angers rage couldn't gage or survey
the pain that remains when there's only one.

Temper words to avoid that instant break
when a feather's weight brings on an earthquake

On our 60th wedding anniversary

I take the pad
off my night table
quietly,
settle in as I sit
down on my soft sheets.
I write *"I love you"*
on the first page,
then tap my pencil.
The quiet blend of humidity's
summer air hangs around me
I wonder how to tell you
how happy I've been
living with you

a smile comes over me
recalling your face,
the day we married,
scared, and nervous
we grew together.

time ages our love
into a unique bouquet whose taste
we easily recognize.
60 years with my favorite book

to enjoy my re-reading slowly,
to savor parts which I remember.
ignoring my trespass of thinking
different is better when time
shows to all you are my true love.

lovers are the caretakers of age
gently holding each other's hearts.

Value of A Man

"Be a man my son" I often would hear
from one on his way out to begin work
there, is where men have their value not here,
here, is where they leave to have to go back.

A magical place where, fathers stay hidden
won't know what you've done
you'll just wait with the threat of their return
under covers 'till sleep stops their mission.

"Be a man, join in, be one of the boys"
as you become a partner's love of choice
surprised to find my father waiting there
nervously, for some grandchildren to snare.

Wisdom learned while hoping for sustenance
a woman's breast was my first influence.

Time to Dream

Solitude stalks your suburban sidewalks
as memories struggle for their recall
hints from whisps of scents feel so minuscule
as you try to open your keepsake's box

unable to stroll on a natural path
amongst the beauty displayed once you'd
partake,
like a bee: you'd search there for life's intake,
sadly tired, all that's left-— a sunbath

to warm your old bones whose early repose
offers at last harmony while you doze
not alone but with your dream fantasy
those past spirits seen from antiquity

kept alive in your dreams where you can hold
on to beauty and a love once bestowed

Secrets Can Hurt

to love is to protect from any harm
and trespasses should be kept well-hidden
if unable, learn to ring an alarm
all say never start to share your passion

men can be victims too when they're surprised
afraid force is not the way to respond
when pleasure controls beyond their command
unable to return once compromised

guilt is such a heavy stone they'll carry
to place it down allows all to see, know
then, cuckold men use their anger's arrow
when trust is unbuckled, both feel empty

secrets should be kept fastened forever
or they'll sting painfully if they untether

Chocolate Cake

you often want the one you shouldn't take
forbidden always looks like the sweetest
remember what happens with chocolate cake

afterwords you'll know it was a mistake
to polish off more than you can digest
you often want the one you shouldn't take

dipped a piece into the coldest milkshake
soggy soaked soft gulps help as you ingest
remember what happens with chocolate cake

bloated from an unnatural intake
stretched stomach pain pushes for time to rest
you often want the one you shouldn't take

your belly rumbles sound like an earthquake
as thoughts of more sweets now, makes you feel
    stress
remember what happens with chocolate cake

as your glazed eyes stare at your high piled plate
you try to recall which bite could cause this
you often want the one you shouldn't take
remember what happens with chocolate cake

About the Author

Bill's love affair with poetry began with strict forms like sonnets. Currently he is focused on poems from daily life. He loves to show history has not changed us. His previous book *Sonnets and More* explores various themes of love relationships. He shows many sides of love with his book *Ways of Love* Published by Prolific Pulse Press and his *Draw of Love* published by Ravens Quote Press. He continues to appear in several other anthologies. His books are available where online books are sold, i.e., Barnes & Noble, Amazon, and other online stores.

Roberta Batorsky is a poet, science journalist, and college educator. She has been writing poetry for about 5 years. She is in several online and in person poetry and fiction writing groups and is putting a poetry book together.
RobertaBatorsky_poetry (Instagram)

www.ingramcontent.com/pod-product-compliance
Lightning Source LLC
Chambersburg PA
CBHW020732310726
48969CB00003B/810

9 781962 374514